The Scary Dinosaur and The Stinky Skunk: A Fable on Accepting Differences and Making New Friends written by D.M. Whitaker and Duce Whitaker

ISBN: 978-1-7357327-0-1

Cataloging-in-Publication Data is on file at the Library of Congress

Library of Congress Control Number: TXu 2-217-369

To Duce and Elisha:

Always be kind to others, try new adventures,
follow your dreams, and remember that you are
fearfully and wonderfully made.

-Mommy

The Scary Dinosaur
and
The Stinky Skunk

A Fable on Accepting Differences and Making New Friends

Story By
D.M. Whitaker with Duce Whitaker

Once upon a time there was a Scary Dinosaur and a Stinky Skunk. They each lived in the woods with their mommy, daddy and baby brother.

The Scary Dinosaur would not play with the Stinky Skunk because she stunk.

The Stinky Skunk was scared of the Scary Dinosaur, but she wanted a new friend.

One day, the Stinky Skunk was sniffing the ground and bumped into the Scary Dinosaur.

The Stinky Skunk sprayed him and ran!

The next day, the Stinky Skunk tiptoed by the Scary Dinosaur. "Roar! Get away from me you Stinky Skunk!" yelled the Scary Dinosaur.

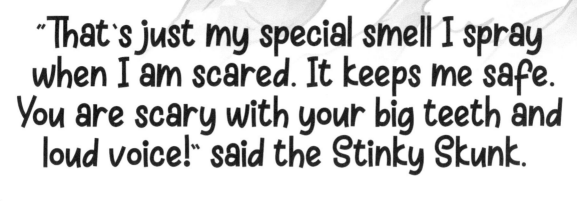

"That's just my special smell I spray when I am scared. It keeps me safe. You are scary with your big teeth and loud voice!" said the Stinky Skunk.

"But that's just my special voice. It keeps me safe, and my teeth help me eat trees and vegetables," said the Scary Dinosaur.

"I have a great idea!" said the Scary Dinosaur excitedly.

"Please don't eat me! Please don't eat me!" said the Stinky Skunk as she covered her eyes.

"No! I want to be best friends Stinky Skunk!" said the Scary Dinosaur.

"But you said I stink. So how can we be best friends?" cried the Stinky Skunk.

"I will have my mom make me a mask to wear! That way I cannot smell your sprays," said the Scary Dinosaur.

"That's a great idea!"
said the Stinky Skunk excitedly.

The Scary Dinosaur and the Stinky Skunk became best friends. They ate trees and vegetable sticks from the Scary Dinosaur's house and the Stinky Skunk's mommy made them peanut butter and jelly sandwiches.

They played with trains...

...and blocks.

They even played tag throughout
the woods.

"Tag you're it!" yelled the Stinky Skunk.

"Tag you're it!" yelled the Scary Dinosaur.

And they played hide and seek!

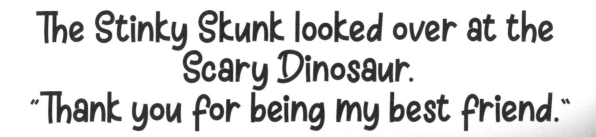

The Stinky Skunk looked over at the
Scary Dinosaur.
"Thank you for being my best friend."

"You are my best friend too!"
said the Scary Dinosaur smiling.

The moral of the Scary Dinosaur and Stinky Skunk's story is: No matter how different you are, you can always find a friend that will love you just the way you are... fearfully and wonderfully made.

~Psalms 139:14

D.M. Whitaker was born in Omaha, Nebraska to a mom and dad that loved reading books to her and her siblings.Thus,her love for reading and sharing those same traditions with her dear sons have been valuable and instrumental in their development. Inspired by being a mother and educator, D.M. loves to write children's books and rhymes that will sketch beautiful memories in children's hearts and inspire them to be their best every day.

D.M. Whitaker currently resides in San Antonio, Texas with her husband Brandon and dear sons, Brandon, II, affectionately known as "Duce" and Elisha. She enjoys being a wife, mother, author, blogger and momprenuer. For more about D.M.,visit her website at : hersheymommychronicles.com and follow her on Instagram @queenq_writes.

Duce Whitaker is an active 3 year old with a vivid imagination full of stories that he loves to create and share at bedtime. Duce enjoys listening and singing along to his favorite playlists, as he plays with his dinosaurs, trains, monster trucks and cars with his baby brother Elisha, who he lovingly calls his best friend.